Don't Touch That Dial!

Out in the van, the lieutenant and Scully watched as the camera panned hard to the left. The room whipped by in a black and white blur. The camera settled on the distorted face of a smirking Robert Modell. Scully could make out the large satin-nickel Colt Python pointed directly at Mulder's head. The camera attempted to adjust its autofocus, but, before it could, Scully saw Modell's hand reach up toward Mulder's head.

White static filled the screen of the TV monitor.

Scully bolted from her chair, terror filling her face. For all she knew, Mulder might already be dead.

Other X-Files books in this series

Voyager

T H E (X) F I L E S ™

Control

Novelization by Everett Owens

Based on the television series
The X-Files created by
Chris Carter

Based on the teleplay
written by Vince Gilligan

HarperCollins*Publishers*

Voyager
An imprint of HarperCollins*Publishers*
77–85 Fulham Palace Road,
Hammersmith, London W6 8JB

This paperback edition 1997
9 8 7 6 5 4 3 2 1

First published in the USA by HarperTrophy
A division of HarperCollins*Publishers* 1997

The X-Files™ © Twentieth Century Fox Film Corporation 1997
All rights reserved

ISBN 0 00 648330 5

Set in Goudy

Printed and bound in Great Britain by
Caledonian International Book Manufacturing Ltd, Glasgow

Chapter One

FBI agent Will Collins set a half gallon of Breyers Dutch Chocolate in his shopping cart without taking his eyes off the murder suspect across the freezer aisle. As his suspect loaded Foodland's entire stock of CarboBoost High Energy Protein Drink into a basket, the young agent priced Eggos and worked his way close enough to hear the man humming along with the store's Muzak.

Once he'd depleted the shelf, the humming man strolled to the end of the express checkout line. Collins paused before moving into line behind him. In front of the humming man, another FBI agent in street clothes waited to pay for a loaf of bread and a magazine.

The humming man—now sandwiched

between the two larger men—set down his basket and took a copy of the *Weekly World Informer* from its rack. A grainy photo of an elongated, hollow-eyed face dominated the cover. The headline announced proof of life on other planets. The man stopped humming momentarily and chuckled. As he looked up, he spotted the red and blue lights of a police car moving like a shark's fin above the roofs of the other cars in the parking lot. For the first time, his expression changed. Though he kept grinning, his smile took on a nasty look that hadn't been there a moment before.

"Let's get this show on the road," he said to no one in particular.

Then he reached up and grabbed the rectangular panel on the back of the jacket of the man standing in front of him and yanked. Velcro gave way. In the space previously covered by the flap, the initials *FBI* were visible.

As if that was their cue, the FBI agents flanking the man grabbed his arms and forced his head down onto the checkout counter. The humming man lay passively as the agents cuffed him. Other shoppers gawked as several more agents moved in with their weapons drawn, shouting, "Federal agents! Get down!"

Before any of the shoppers could panic, the arrest was over. *Textbook*, Agent Collins thought to himself.

The electric doors of the store swung open and agent-in-charge Frank Burst, a barrel-chested bureau veteran in his late forties, strode in.

"You're Pusher, I presume," he said, noting the features of the handcuffed, thirty-ish, white male pinned to the counter in front of him.

The prisoner had to roll his eyes upward to see who was talking to him. Then he smiled crookedly.

"You must be Frank Burst," he said. "I gotta tell you—I think you've got a great name."

Burst was used to criminals with attitude. He knew better than to give Pusher the sat-isfaction of getting under his skin.

"Agent Collins," he said to the young

agent who had tailed Pusher through the store. "Read him his rights, and let's get him out of here."

Collins pulled Pusher up from the counter and began reciting his Mirandas as he steered him toward the door. A procession of local police and FBI agents surrounded the man.

"Think you can hold me?" Pusher taunted.

Despite the group setting, it was obvious that he was directing his gibe at Burst. It was an implied threat Burst took very seriously.

"I want him in a waist chain and leg irons. I want him in a car with a cage: Loudon County unit, whatever. I'll ride shotgun."

The extra precautions didn't seem to impress Pusher. He appeared nonchalant as he was led through a crowd of gaping bystanders.

Seven cars were charged with transporting him to a holding cell. Burst rode in the last car while a sheriff's deputy did the driving. Inconveniently for Burst, the arrest had taken place just as afternoon rush-hour traffic began to clog the streets of Loudon County,

Virginia. Ahead of him, the first three patrol cars waited to turn left from a feeder road onto a busy highway. It was taking longer than Burst would have liked. Behind him, on the other side of a steel screen, sat Pusher.

"You know," said Burst, "it'd really help me out if you told us your name."

The man shrugged and gazed down the road to his left.

"Pusher's good enough," he said before shifting his attention to the driver. "Deputy? I just gotta say. Your uniform is the most soothing shade of blue."

The deputy snorted and pulled up as the car ahead of him was finally able to turn left.

"No, I'm not kidding you," Pusher continued. "I notice these things. It's sort of a sky blue. Very calming . . . tranquil. I think the word for that particular shade is 'cerulean,' actually."

Burst decided there was something in Pusher's voice he didn't like. Something about its quietness, the soothing quality. Burst glanced over at the deputy and decided he wasn't paying any attention.

"Okay, we get it—it's a nice shade of blue," Burst said as he looked out restlessly at the oncoming cars. "What's with this traffic?"

The man in the backseat kept staring out the left-side window. A small bead of sweat formed at his hairline and slid down his temple.

"Cerulean blue," he said, even softer this time.

Traffic remained heavy on the highway when it was time to turn left. Cars zoomed by. There was a gap, room enough to make it . . . possibly, except for a light-blue eighteen-wheeler rumbling up the highway filling the space.

"Cerulean blue makes me think of a breeze," came the voice from the backseat. "A gentle breeze . . ."

By now Burst was irritated.

"Hey," he snapped, "put a sock in it."

"Cerulean is a gentle breeze," Pusher continued, ignoring Burst. His attention was focused on the deputy.

Inside the deputy's head, Pusher's words

were reverberating. The deputy could swear he felt a gentle breeze, even though he was vaguely aware of the fact that all the windows were rolled up. The deputy blinked, and the semi that had been preventing him from turning was gone. The roar of the diesel engine was gone as well. All he could hear was the soothing sound of that cool, cerulean breeze as he pulled out onto the highway.

In the backseat, Pusher spun and braced his legs hard against the passenger-side door. Burst turned just in time to see the deputy's serene smile and the front grille of a semi filling up the driver's-side window.

"Stop!" Burst screamed.

Its air horn blaring, the eighteen-wheeler locked its brakes and skidded into the patrol car. The last thing Burst saw before losing consciousness was the company logo painted above the top of the semi's windshield. The type spelled out *Cerulean*.

Chapter Two

An image projected on the screen showed the deputy belly-down on the asphalt. Blood ran away from the body like streams from a lake. Agent Burst, his face swollen and bruised, his nose obviously broken, a series of lacerations on his cheek and neck just beginning to heal, narrated for agents Fox Mulder and Dana Scully.

"When the truck hit us, I was knocked unconscious. Deputy Scott Kerber was mortally injured," Burst said. "But before he succumbed, he managed to crawl out of the car and dig his keys from his pocket. His last breath was spent unlocking the prisoner, who, despite his own injuries, managed to escape on foot."

As he continued talking, Agent Burst

became visibly angrier but managed not to raise his voice.

"The guy calls himself 'Pusher,' " he added.

Agent Mulder tapped the eraser of his pencil against his temple.

"What's his story?"

"He cold-called me about a month ago," Burst replied. "Confessed to a string of contract killings going back two years."

"He wanted to turn himself in?" Agent Scully asked.

"No, not at all. He was bragging," said Burst. "It's all a game to him. The thing of it is, no one seems to think these murders of his were murders at all. They all went on the books as suicides."

Agent Scully attempted to make sense of what she was hearing.

"So this man is a crank?"

Burst knew what he was saying was out of the ordinary. He also knew that was the reason he'd been directed to Mulder and Scully. Everyone at the bureau had heard of the strange and unexplained cases thrown into the X-files.

"No. He knows too much about each case," Burst explained, "too many details that were only in the police reports."

By now Mulder was intrigued. What had started out looking like a simple escape had suddenly become more interesting. He leaned forward in his chair. Scully continued to probe for the logical solution.

"What connection did this dead deputy have with him?"

"None, as far as I can tell. Kerber was a good cop."

"Then why did Kerber free him?" Scully asked.

Burst paused. This was the part of the interview he knew they'd get to, but his only theory violated everything ingrained in him by years of law enforcement work. He advanced the next slide. The new photograph showed the front of the blue semi.

"Pusher was rambling on about cerulean blue. Talking about how it reminded him of a breeze or something." Burst searched his memory. "He kept repeating 'Cerulean is a gentle breeze.' Over and over. Right then, Kerber pulls in front of the truck."

"Blammo."

Burst clicked to the next slide. This one was a close-up of the "Cerulean Hauling— Coast 2 Coast" logo painted on the cab. Mulder turned his attention away from the screen and faced Burst.

"So you're saying he talked him into it? Somehow willed him to do it?"

"Willed him?" Scully repeated doubtfully. "How?"

"No kidding—how?" Burst echoed, shaking his head. "I'm not sure *what* I'm saying. I don't have much experience with this sort of thing. I just want to catch the guy."

Burst hit the remote control again and a new slide came up. Fingerpainted in a bloody scrawl above the fender wheelwell of the smashed patrol car were the letters NIN OR.

"Your guess is as good as mine on this one," Burst said.

Mulder studied the image. He stood and

walked over to the slide projector. He ejected the slide, turned it around, and dropped it back in. The image that now appeared on screen was reversed.

Burst remained unimpressed.

"Ro Nin. So what?"

"Rho-*neen*," Mulder said, correcting Burst's pronunciation. "A samurai without a master."

Scully gaped at Mulder, who returned her look of incredulity with a shrug. "What? You never saw *Yojimbo?*"

"Still," Scully said, "what does it mean?"

"It means ten to one I know what this guy's got stacked on the back of his toilet."

Chapter Three

Holly Patton, the FBI researcher who brought a pile of the past five years' issues of *American Ronin* magazine to Mulder's office, didn't even bother to ask what they were for. She didn't want to know. She'd seen a number of strange requests come down from the X-files offices in her months on the job. *All in all*, she thought to herself, *this one's less odd than most.*

Mulder and Scully divided the pile into two. They weren't even sure what they were looking for, but Mulder was confident there was a clue to be found in the magazines.

"Oh, look," Scully said, pointing to the cover of the first issue. "How to sniper-proof your home."

"I just get it for the pictures," Mulder

replied. He flashed Scully a photo of a bikini-clad woman caressing a smoking Uzi.

Hours later, Scully had several pages of notes jotted down on a legal pad. Mulder's memory was photographic, so although he wasn't jotting down notes as Scully was, he was slowly scanning each page for clues. When Holly Patton returned with a fresh stack of magazines, she could tell the agents were both deeply engrossed in their work.

"Agents," she said shyly, not wanting to interrupt, "here's volume ten."

Scully glanced up and noticed a nasty bruise on Holly's cheek and forehead. Holly shifted uncomfortably when she felt Scully staring at her.

"I'm sorry . . . I couldn't help noticing," Scully said.

Holly had told the story so many times in the past two days, she was tired of it. "I was in Georgetown this weekend," she said. "A guy knocked me down and stole my purse."

Scully murmured her regrets; Mulder, naturally, wanted details.

"Did they catch him?" he asked.

"Do they ever?" Holly replied without thinking. "I mean . . . no offense."

Holly forced a smile, but the mugging still had her jumpy. She didn't need to be reminded of it. She headed out the door wondering whether there was a way she could wear her hair that might cover up the bruises. Mulder turned his attention back to the magazines while Scully's eyes lingered on the door. When she looked down, she saw Mulder had slid another four issues onto her stack.

"Mulder, I'm still not sure what we're searching for."

Mulder didn't glance up.

"Samurais without masters have to advertise—"

"Yeah, but advertise what?" Scully asked, interrupting him. "How did this Pusher convince a supposedly honest deputy sheriff to free him?"

Scully gazed across the table at her partner. A wry smile pushed up the corners of her mouth.

"I'm sure *you* have a theory."

Mulder shrugged. "Suggestion is a powerful force. The science of hypnosis is predicated on it. As are TV commercials. They're specifically designed to plant thoughts in our heads."

"Inducing someone to buy soap," Scully pointed out, "is not the same as convincing them to pull in front of a speeding truck."

"But the mechanism of suggestion is the same. In this case it's just more powerful." Mulder decided to share more of his theory with his partner. "This guy calls himself 'Pusher.' Can't we take that to mean he pushes his will onto others?"

The premise didn't hold up for Scully.

"Mulder, even if he *could* 'push' his will, why would he cause an accident while he himself was in the car?"

Mulder's expression indicated he hadn't worked that part out yet. "I guess he *really* didn't want to go to jail." He shrugged, then circled something in the magazine with his highlighter pen.

"Look at this." He pointed to the circled

classified ad and read it out loud.

I SOLVE PROBLEMS. OSU. (703) 555-0145; (703) 555-0118; (703) 555-0177.

"O-S-U? Ohio State University?" Scully asked.

"I don't think so," Mulder replied. "It's a northern Virginia area code. I've seen this ad in every issue dating back to April 1994."

"The time span of the murders," said Scully.

"O-S-U . . . " Mulder said musingly. He stood and began pacing back and forth in front of the reference shelves that lined the dimly lit office. He recited the letters like a mantra. "O . . . S . . . U, O . . . S . . . U . . . " Then he stopped dead. Something had caught his eye. He pulled down the Japanese-English dictionary and began thumbing through it.

"O-S-U. *Osu.*" He looked up at Scully. "The Japanese verb 'to push.'"

Mulder and Scully stared at each other. They knew this was their man. Scully was the first to speak.

"I say we run down those numbers."

Mulder slapped the book closed.

Chapter Four

The commuter parking lot outside Falls Church, Virginia, had been deserted for hours. Streetlamps illuminated the two FBI agents occupying the front seat of an unmarked sedan. Mulder slouched behind the wheel, wishing they weren't so conspicuous, but they needed a clear view of the pay phone—whose number was one of the three in the *American Ronin* ad. Next to Mulder, Scully dozed, her head gradually sagging and resting lightly on his shoulder. Mulder glanced at his partner but didn't wake her. Instead he withdrew his cell phone from his pocket and used his thumb to speed dial.

A moment later the pay phone across the parking lot began to ring. Mulder let it do so five or six times before sighing and hanging up. As he flipped the phone closed, he tapped Scully's head. She awakened quickly, embarrassed to find she had been using Mulder as a pillow. She shook her head to clear the cobwebs.

"I think you drooled on me," Mulder teased.

Scully stretched, then glanced out the window toward the pay phone.

"Um. Sorry. What time is it?"

"Twenty till three," Mulder said.

"No luck, I take it?"

"No, nothing here. Nothing at the other two pay phones. I checked in with Burst. He's beginning to think it's a wild-goose chase."

As he finished his sentence, they heard the faint ringing of the pay phone across the parking lot.

"That's not you?" Scully asked.

Mulder checked to make sure he hadn't accidentally speed dialed his cellular. He shook his head. The two agents scrambled out of the car and sprinted across the asphalt toward the phone. It was still ringing when they reached it. Mulder lifted the receiver.

"Hello?" he said, flipping on his miniature tape recorder.

"Are you two just gonna sit there all night?" asked the voice on the other end. Mulder pointed at Scully, indicating they had their man. Scully whipped out her own cell phone to call for a trace.

"Don't bother hunting around for me," the voice continued. "I'm far away. Though I was watching you up until about an hour ago."

Mulder thought the killer on the other end of the line seemed awfully pleased with himself, but he let him go on.

"You and your pretty partner seem awfully close. Do you work well together?"

"Who's asking?" Mulder bent down to allow Scully to share the earpiece with him. "What's your name?"

"Sorry, G-Man. It's not that easy. You have to follow my little bread-crumb trail . . . prove your worth. So far," the voice continued, "you're doing all right."

Mulder considered ways of baiting Pusher into staying on the line until the trace went through. "Why do I have to prove my worth to you?" he asked. "Is this a game to you? Do you want to be found?"

There was no response, so Mulder continued.

"So . . . where's my next bread crumb?"

"Right in front of you. Let your fingers do the walking, G-Man."

Then Mulder heard a click, followed by a dial tone. Pusher had hung up. Scully listened to her cell phone, spoke a few words that Mulder couldn't hear, then snapped it shut.

"No complete trace," she said. "They think he was using a digital scrambler."

Mulder nodded, but his mind was elsewhere.

"Let your fingers do the walking . . . " he repeated.

"The phone book?" Scully suggested.

Mulder pointed to the hanging binder. The phone book that was supposed to be inside was missing. That couldn't be it. Their eyes focused on the phone itself.

"Who was the last person to use this phone?" Mulder asked. "What if it was him?"

Scully considered the idea. She punched the button on her cell phone that got her the FBI communication center.

"It's me again," she told the operator. "I need the last number dialed out from this location. Just ring it back through."

Scully turned off her cell phone, and she and Mulder waited. The pay phone gave the short double rings that indicated a return call. Scully picked it up and, returning the favor, allowed Mulder to listen in. On the other end a machine answered. The voice was female and very Southern.

"Hi, you've reached Tee-Totalers golf driving range and pro shop! Our hours of operation are seven A.M. to midnight, Monday through . . . "

The recorded message rambled on, but Scully had already taken the phone away from her ear. She turned to Mulder.

"So he's a killer and a golfer," she said.

Mulder smiled.

"Rings a bell," he said. "Let's go, G-Woman."

Chapter Five

Akio Ohga didn't understand Americans. Even though he spoke the language fluently and had spent a year in the United States, he was still baffled by the American psyche. The gentleman before him was a perfect example. Ohga and his associates had come to the driving range for relaxation, a chance to take a break from the tensions of business. Had they more time, they probably would have gotten in eighteen holes.

When the American had approached and asked if he could join them, Ohga's first instinct was to point out that his party was the only one hitting balls at the Tee-Totalers range. The American could choose any of two dozen empty tee boxes if he so wished. The distinctively American gall of the man was offensive to Ohga. Still, there was something in the way the man asked. Something compelling in his voice. Before Ohga knew what he was doing, he heard the words "It would be our pleasure" coming out of his mouth. The American had bowed in return and thanked him. *In Japanese*, no less!

Ohga stepped up to the ball, took a deep breath, and attempted to clear his mind. He found this surprisingly easy to do. His focus on the golf ball seemed absolute. He kept his backswing slow. The hitch that normally occurred when he brought the club above his head had miraculously vanished. His swing was fluid. When he struck the ball, he knew without looking up that the shot was a thing of beauty.

"Good ball!" said the American. *So loud, the American. But friendly.* That was another quality common to the people Ohga met in his travels here. "Strong ball!" the American added.

The striped range ball stopped rolling just

past the 225-yard marker. *Not a bad shot for a four-iron*, Ohga thought to himself. The American stepped up to the tee out of turn. None of the men mentioned his breach of etiquette. Pusher spoke.

"All right. I'm using this nonsanctioned ball. It's got a core of damn uranium or something—I don't know what. It gets up there like Sputnik."

Ohga took a moment to appraise the American as he would a business rival. Nothing extraordinary about his looks: like so many American men, he was a bit soft around the middle and dressed inappropriately, in a pullover sweatshirt, blue jeans, and high-top tennis shoes. Brown-haired and blue-eyed. Not especially tall. Ohga guessed him to be in his mid-thirties. Normally Ohga would dismiss him as a lifetime junior executive, but there was something extraordinary in his demeanor—the American both demanded and commanded attention. His aggressive pursuit of it, Ohga decided, was what stood out most.

Pusher waggled his two-iron and squinted as he surveyed the driving range. Then he saw it. A piece of glass, movement maybe. Something reflecting the sun at the tree-lined edge of the driving range.

"About damn time," Pusher muttered to himself. He'd begun to believe he might be forced to draw a map for the feds, maybe fax it to FBI headquarters. Then, twenty minutes ago or so, he'd started picking up something that he could only describe as the mental scent of hunters.

But Pusher wasn't about to let the cavalry interrupt his golf just when he'd found worthy Japanese partners—men who understood the art of competition. He decided to play on, even if just for a few more minutes.

Three hundred yards away at the tree line, two federal SWAT cops moved like smoke, low to the ground, their rifles slung across their backs as they worked their way into a clear shot at their target. The pair wore full gillie suits, with grass-and-twigs camouflage making them nearly invisible to each other.

There was no way they could have known they had already been spotted.

Pusher didn't worry much about form when he golfed. He figured he routinely tacked on another twenty yards through sheer attitude. With the Japanese businessmen serving as his gallery, he brought his backswing up with a jerk and grunted like Jimmy Connors as he powered his clubhead through the ball. He didn't stop, though, to watch it fly. Instead he turned and gave a slight bow to his partners.

"*Konnichiwa*, gentlemen," he said. "I was never here."

Then he grabbed his golf bag and moved rapidly away. The four Japanese businessmen stared vacantly at one another. None of them could seem to remember whose turn it was. From the far end of the driving range, one of the SWAT men saw the foursome arguing as he tried to pick out Pusher in his scope. He had no luck finding his target, but he was nearly struck by a golf ball that rolled right up to his position.

Three more SWAT cops in black protective uniforms and masks were already cutting through the hedges and service buildings that made up the Tee-Totalers complex. They had been briefed two hours earlier. The man they were after had been responsible for a number of deaths, at least one that of a cop. Holding their MP5Ks out in front of them, they moved stealthily around the grounds. When they reached the corner of the clubhouse, the team leader silently hand-signaled the other two and the trio split up. As he rounded a corner, the leader spotted a groundskeeper's shed with a door slightly ajar. He moved into position, with his back pressed up against the tin wall alongside the door. Sucking in a deep breath, he launched himself through the opening. He saw the figure. Most of the body was in darkness, but a beam of light streaming in through a fan vent cut across the man's torso.

The cop barked orders with authority.

"Freeze! Get down!"

He already had the red laser targeting

device centered on the suspect's heart. The man had put his hands in the air without being told, but the way the light fell, the cop was unable to see the man's face.

"Whoa . . . whoa . . . whoa. Okay. Okay," Pusher answered, though he made no move to get down on the floor. "Relax," he told the cop. "*Relax.*"

The SWAT man didn't want to relax. He wanted to pull the trigger. Drop the cop killer. The man wasn't getting on the floor like he was supposed to. Didn't he see the assault rifle? Didn't he see the red dot of light hovering around his heart? So why couldn't the SWAT man do it? The rules of engagement told him he could fire . . . at least shoot him in the shoulder, the right shoulder, put him on the ground. The target wasn't doing what he was told.

"Let me see your face," Pusher said as he took a step toward the light. Now the cop could see his eyes. The light made Pusher's face seem to glow, and the cop found he couldn't look away. The last thing he wanted to do was show the killer his face, but he couldn't stop himself. He could still think. He was still aware of what he was doing, but there was a more powerful will than his own at work in his head. He stood there horrified, painfully conscious that his arms and hands were obeying someone else's whim. The red dot sank lower and lower until it pointed away from Pusher and down toward the cop's own feet. Off came his helmet. He heard it clatter on the cement floor of the shed. It stopped rolling next to one of the riding lawn-mowers.

"That's right," said Pusher. "Take it easy."

The cop's hands reached for the black nylon mask that covered his entire head and face, with only a hole for his eyes.

Pusher recognized the cop even before the mask was all the way off. It was the same presence he'd felt the last time he'd shopped for groceries—the cop who'd read him his rights. What was his name? He searched for it, and found it without much effort.

"Hey, Collins," Pusher said. A bead of

sweat rolled down his temple, but he spoke like an old friend asking a simple favor. "Listen. First I need you to do something for me."

With his toe, Pusher moved a gallon can of gasoline a couple of feet closer to Collins.

"Will you do something for me?" Pusher asked, casting a dark smile at Collins.

Outside, Mulder, Scully and Burst patrolled the complex with their guns drawn. Scully rounded the clubhouse and was the first to see it. Her eyes went wide at the scene unfolding in front of her.

"Mulder!" she called, but by then Mulder had spotted it too.

They watched as Agent Collins trudged down the middle of a sidewalk. Drenched with gasoline, he was carrying the can upside down under one arm, the gas guggling down the side of his body. As he came closer into view, Scully and Mulder could see droplets of the liquid running off his nose and hair. Collins's eyes were already swollen from exposure to the gasoline. His lips quivered.

"Collins?" Mulder shouted.

"What the hell?" said Burst.

Collins moved like a robot, a drunk robot. Stiff and awkward.

"Oh God," he sobbed. "Oh God."

He squeezed the can under his arm. The steel pinged and began to crumple. He changed direction, and Mulder, Scully, and Burst were able to see what Collins held in his other hand: a butane lighter. Collins raised it.

The other agents found themselves briefly paralyzed, unsure of what they should do. They watched as Collins clicked the lighter. There was a brief spark, but no flame. A huge sob racked Collins's body.

"Stop me," he begged.

Scully had to force herself to quit being a spectator. She realized that tackling Collins might only result in two casualties. She remembered a fire extinguisher hanging behind the snack bar in the clubhouse. She sprinted toward the building. Mulder began taking off his jacket. He and Agent Burst were just a few feet from Collins, who held the lighter out in front of him and clicked it again.

"Collins, what the hell are you doing?" Burst repeated.

Collins didn't answer. He kept the lighter between himself and his two superiors.

"Let it go," Mulder commanded. "Put it down!"

But Collins clicked the lighter again. This time a tall blue flame sprang up and flickered menacingly. Collins squeezed his eyes shut. Inside his brain he was fighting a battle that he knew he was losing. He struggled to regain control of his body, his arms, his legs, but the best he could manage was to shake his head in a terrified no as his hand brought the flame up to his chest.

Collins was consumed in fire almost instantaneously.

Scully was twenty yards away when he became a pillar of flame. She aimed the extinguisher and doused him in white CO_2 powder. Mulder flung his coat over the smoking SWAT cop and tackled him, patting out what was left of the flames. Scully dropped to her knees and began attending to Collins. She ripped open his melted web gear and body armor, burning her own hands.

Collins twitched and convulsed almost as if he was having a seizure—a reaction, Scully noted, that seemed unrelated to his injuries. His hair was gone for the most part, and the flesh of his face was falling away where it wasn't blistering. Scully knew he was in shock. His head rocked from side to side as he kept repeating, "Light up . . . light up . . . light up."

Burst was barking orders into his cell phone.

"Get me a burn unit! Now! Yeah . . . bad. Real bad. Get someone over here now!"

Mulder felt helpless. This was Scully's specialty, and he knew it. He stared at Collins's charred body, amazed by what he had just witnessed. As he was staring, he became aware of a car horn honking some-where nearby. He spotted a lone car, a Cadillac, at the far end of the parking lot.

He walked a few steps, then broke into a run. Two of the other SWAT cops followed. Mulder approached the car from behind, from what he knew would be a driver's blind spot. He grabbed the door handle and yanked it open. His gun was drawn in his other hand.

"Federal agents!" he shouted above the horn.

Pusher was in the driver's seat. His head rested against the steering wheel, causing the horn to blow. Mulder pushed his head back. The horn died, and Mulder heard words that made his blood run cold.

"Light up . . . light up . . . light up," Pusher repeated.

Mulder had seen junkies who looked better than Pusher at that moment. The man was fish-belly white and dripping with sweat, panting as if he'd just finished a marathon. His eyes were rolled back into his head. Somehow he drew the energy to open his eyes and smile weakly at Mulder.

"Five bucks says I get off," he whispered.

Chapter Six

The preliminary hearing was held at the relatively modern Alexandria District Courthouse. A number of the SWAT cops—buddies of Collins's who had just come from visiting him at the hospital—nearly filled the small gallery. The jury box was empty. In Virginia, judges decided in their own preliminary trials whether there was enough evidence to hold a suspect.

Agent Burst sat down next to the prosecuting attorney as the bailiff instructed Pusher to stand and state his name and address for the court. Pusher rose at the next table and faced the judge.

"Robert Patrick Modell, 3083 Roseneath Avenue, Apartment 9, Alexandria, Virginia," he said confidently.

Mulder sat in the second row of the gallery with Scully. He always was surprised how nicely some of the criminals they brought to trial cleaned up. If only the judge could have seen the sweaty, arrogant killer Mulder had caught in the Cadillac. Here in the courtroom, wearing a suit and acting contrite, Pusher looked more like an insurance salesman than a sociopath.

Mulder, as the arresting officer, was one of the first witnesses called to testify. The middle-aged judge, renowned locally for his efficiency, asked Mulder preliminary questions.

"Agent Mulder, does the FBI believe that this defendant is responsible for fourteen murders?"

"That is correct, Your Honor," Mulder responded.

The judge's eyebrows furrowed as he studied the file in front of him.

"In each of the cases the coroner's office ruled for suicide."

It wasn't really a question, but Mulder felt he should speak.

"We believe they were indeed murders, Your Honor."

"You believe?" the judge said doubtfully. "But do you have any evidence?"

As he responded, Mulder kept his eyes fixed on the man he now knew as Robert Patrick Modell.

"We have the defendant on audiotape confessing to the murders on several separate occasions. He clearly identifies them as such. Furthermore, the defendant knows crime scene details that are only available to police." Mulder switched his gaze to the judge. "And finally, Your Honor, in none of those fourteen cases had a victim been suffering from depression. None of the victims had been seeing a psychiatrist. Not one of them left a note. And none of them had ever attempted suicide before. They were hardly what we think of as classic suicide cases."

At the end of the defense table, Agent Burst gave a seconding nod. Modell's defense attorney, a well-respected public defender in her forties, glanced down at her folder. "Your

Honor, one of these so-called murder victims threw herself under a commuter train," she said. "This was on a crowded platform, in front of a hundred witnesses. Nobody pushed her. No one was within thirty feet of her."

Scully watched the proceedings knowing the defender had the weight of logic behind her. Mulder didn't back down.

"But your client was present . . ."

"Which is how he knew your crime scene details," the defender broke in.

The judge leaned forward, anxious to hear whether the FBI had any more of a case.

"Make your point, Agent Mulder."

"I believe," Mulder began, "that those people died because it was Mr. Modell's express will that they do so."

The judge wasn't sure he'd heard Mulder right.

"His will?"

Scully looked down at the floor, shaking her head. Masking his incredulity, the prosecuting attorney examined a loose thread on his tie. Mulder knew his best bet to impress the judge was to appear unruffled and dead serious.

"This man admitted to being a killer for hire. I believe he has a unique suggestive ability which makes for the perfect M.O.—he talks his victims into injuring themselves. He overrides their wills with his own."

The defense attorney allowed herself to smile.

"I don't believe this!" she said in a tone that indicated amusement and disbelief.

The judge peered over the top of his glasses at Mulder.

"You wanna run that by me again, Agent Mulder?"

Mulder decided to play his best card.

"Yesterday, a federal law enforcement officer was induced to self-immolation by the defendant. I witnessed it." Mulder pointed out Scully, Burst, and the SWAT cops in the gallery. "All of these officers witnessed it."

Burst noticed the agents in the gallery had grown uncomfortable as soon as they became potential witnesses. But he had worked too hard on this case to give up.

"We have Modell's confession!" Burst shouted out of turn.

The young prosecutor sitting next to Burst touched the agent's arm, gently silencing him. If he was going to save the case, he needed to do it before things got any further out of hand.

"Your Honor, the evidence chain in this case has been difficult to establish," the prosecutor said. "We ask the court's indulgence while we complete our investigation, and that Mr. Modell be held for trial on the strength of his taped confession."

The judge turned his attention to Robert Modell. Regardless of what he thought of the FBI agent's testimony, he realized a confession was probably enough to hold the suspect for a few days.

"What about this audiotape, Mr. Modell?" the judge asked. "*Did* you confess to fourteen murders?"

The defense attorney whispered into

Modell's ear before he spoke, instructing him to keep his answer simple and to tell the truth.

"Unfortunately yes, Your Honor," Modell said, looking ashamed. "Not that I remember it . . ."

His attorney took over.

"This was basically a drunken phone prank on the part of my client, Your Honor."

Mulder was still sitting in the witness stand. Now logic was starting to swing back in his favor.

"Phone prank?" Mulder echoed incredulously. "Your Honor, he knew the details of every case."

Once again, the defense attorney cut Mulder off.

"And Robert deeply regrets the distress and confusion this situation has caused."

From his seat Modell nodded contritely. Behind him the SWAT agents fumed.

Taking in the scene, the judge fixed his gaze on Modell.

"You deny these charges?"

"Absolutely," Modell answered. "I am not guilty."

Mulder watched the exchange closely. He didn't like what he was seeing. The trouble was, he wasn't quite sure *what* he was seeing. The judge's stare when he looked at Modell seemed somehow empty. And what was it with Modell's voice? His answer didn't sound convincing, exactly. It sounded soothing. He talked to the judge like an old friend or an understanding doctor.

Mulder knew the judge's decision before it was out of his mouth.

Chapter Seven

In the hall outside the courtroom, Robert Modell shook hands with his attorney and thanked her for a job well done.

She gave him a victorious pat on the shoulder as he moved past her and began descending the stairs. Mulder, Scully, and Burst had gathered on the landing below him. Smiling, Modell joined the trio as if he were one of the gang.

"I believe you owe me five dollars," he told Mulder.

Mulder whipped out a crisp five-dollar bill, surprising Burst, Scully, and even Modell himself. Mulder glanced down, then looked back up at Modell.

"Your shoe's untied."

Modell involuntarily checked his shoes

before reaching out to take the bill. Mulder snapped it away.

"Made you look," Mulder said.

Modell and Mulder attempted to stare each other down, but neither would look away. Finally Modell smiled crookedly in appreciation. A dumb joke, but Mulder had bent him to his will. Mulder spoke quietly, intently observing Modell.

"So how do *you* do it?"

Modell ignored the question, smiled, and strolled away whistling "Misty." This last act of arrogance was more than Agent Burst could tolerate. He followed him the first couple steps, shouting.

"Hey, Modell! I know your name now! I know where you live!"

But Modell didn't bother to turn around. Scully and Mulder watched their suspect walk away a free man. Burst turned to Mulder as if he intended to say something. He thought better of it and stormed off instead.

Chapter Eight

The FBI firing range was usually deserted during the lunch hour. That's why Mulder liked to go there then. He wanted to be alone to think, and for some reason, wearing heavy-duty earphones and concentrating on a target allowed him to focus even more clearly on the case at hand. The FBI range offered choices in cardboard targets: stock human bad guys in sundry menacing positions or outlined milk bottles that brought to mind Norman Rockwell images of kids with slingshots.

Today Mulder chose the milk bottles. He pressed a button and the motorized target whirred to a distance thirty yards away before chunking to a stop. After inserting a magazine, Mulder drop-closed the slide on his pistol, took aim, and squeezed off eight shots slow and steady. But his eyes were focused beyond the target. He was thinking about Modell . . . Pusher.

Agent Scully approached Mulder from behind, carrying a handful of files. Even though she wasn't shooting, she wore goggles and ear protection. She waited to speak until Mulder stopped to reload.

"I dug up a few more things on our Robert Patrick Modell."

Mulder set down his pistol and pulled off his headphones. He had gotten up early and done this legwork himself.

"Let me guess," he said. "He was an average student, attended an average community college, did an average stint in the military."

Scully was used to Mulder's thoroughness. She played along.

"What branch of the service?" she quizzed.

"The Army—but it wasn't his first choice. He tried to be a Navy Seal. After that, Army Special Forces, then Green Berets. He washed out of all three, though not for lack of intelligence. He wound up a Fort Bragg supply clerk. Served two years. General discharge."

Scully nodded along, waiting until he had finished. "Did you know he applied to the FBI?"

She was pleased to see that this fact surprised Mulder. Occasionally she beat him to the punch.

"He didn't even come close to passing our psych screening," she added.

"You've got a copy?" Mulder asked, amazed.

Scully presented him with a dense two-page report. Mulder scanned it greedily, while she ran down the salient points.

"They found him to be acutely ego-centered. He has no regard for the feelings of others, instead perceiving people as objects. He's extremely suspicious of government and authority."

"Yet he wants to be in a position of authority," Mulder observed.

Scully nodded.

"Our screener caught him in a dozen self-aggrandizing lies: how he was a master of martial arts trained by Gurkhas in Nepal, by ninja in Japan."

"Ninja are said to have the ability to cloud the minds of their opponents," Mulder interjected.

"Are we talking kung fu movies, Mulder?"

"Modell clouded the mind of that judge."

"Mulder, even if Modell could, he didn't need to. We barely had a case against him."

Mulder was good at keeping his feelings to himself—around others he rarely lost his cool—but Scully could tell when he was irritated. He was getting there now. And a bit frustrated.

"We had enough to get past a simple preliminary hearing. Modell put the whammy on him."

"Please explain to me the scientific nature of . . . the whammy," Scully said.

Mulder felt sure he was on the right track, but Scully had a point—he needed to ground his theory in something concrete.

"Maybe we're talking about an Eastern martial art. Maybe a temporary suppression of the brain's chemistry induced by a specific timbre or cadence of Modell's voice. His voice seems to be the key."

Scully shook her head.

"Mulder, Modell's last known employment was as a convenience store clerk. He never studied with ninja. He's never even been outside the U.S. He's just a little man who wishes he were someone big. And we're feeding that wish."

Scully didn't want to embarrass her partner by poking holes in his theory, but she felt she needed to state the case against it.

"And what about that failed psych screening?" she continued. "If Modell could actually control people's minds, right now he'd be an FBI agent. Right? He'd be a Navy Seal, a Green Beret . . ."

But Mulder had an explanation. "Maybe this ability came to him more recently, just in the last two years."

Scully made a skeptical face, which only

annoyed him further.

"Fine," Mulder said. "Give me *your* theory. How did he do what he did to Agent Collins? An otherwise sane family man lights himself on fire! You witnessed it."

Scully sighed. "What do you want me to say, Mulder? That I believe Modell is guilty of murder? I do. Only I'm still looking for explanations a little more mundane than 'the whammy.'"

Mulder holstered his pistol and gathered his shooting gear while he considered her words. He flipped the return switch and the target noisily trundled back to him.

"He's laughing at us, Scully," Mulder said as he yanked down the target.

A tight cluster of eight bullet holes shredded the center of the milk bottle.

Chapter Nine

Anyone can visit the lobby of the J. Edgar Hoover FBI Building in Washington, D.C. The bureau takes a keen interest, however, in what visitors do once they're within those walls. If a visitor desires access to anything more sensitive than the brochures on display at the information desk, he must pass through metal detectors and a phalanx of burly, highly trained security guards.

Robert Patrick Modell entered the building through the swinging glass doors along with a group of secretaries returning from a lunch break. He quickly split from the pack and ducked behind a fat column. There he pulled a business envelope and a marker pen from inside his jacket. Appearing completely unconcerned with the risk he was taking,

Modell scrawled PASS on the envelope in wide black letters. He folded the envelope in half and placed it in the breast pocket of his jacket in such a way that anyone could see it. Then he continued through the lobby to the metal detector. He walked through without setting the machine off.

One of the lobby guards blocked his path. Pusher smiled at the guard, who stared blankly at the "pass" on his lapel. When he looked up, Modell seemed to pin him with his eyes.

"Excuse me," Modell said. "Where might I find the Computer Records Section?"

The question confused the guard. Something was wrong, but he couldn't put his finger on it. Was he supposed to give out this information? Suddenly he wasn't sure.

"F-f-fourth floor," he stammered. "West wing."

"Thank you," Modell said as he moved past the guard toward the elevators.

Once he reached the correct floor, Modell searched the hallway for the correct office. A couple of FBI employees noticed him, but Modell stared at them for a moment, and they paid no further attention. He followed a sign and went through an open door. Inside the office, Holly Patton, her face still not completely healed from the mugging in Georgetown, looked up from her computer.

"Can I help you?" she asked the stranger.

Modell smiled down at her and nodded.

"I need to know some things"—he spotted the nameplate on her desk—"Holly."

Modell began closing the window blinds one by one for privacy. He removed the fake pass from his jacket as Holly continued staring at him. She nodded hesitantly.

"What can I get for you?" she asked.

A few seconds later Holly was tapping keys. On the monitor, a blank screen gave way to a warning page: *The contents of personnel files are the sole property of the Federal Bureau of Investigation. No access without the express authorization of the director.*

"Now," Modell instructed Holly, "if you'll just let me use the keyboard."

Holly vacated her chair, and Modell took her place at the computer. He tapped the keys rapidly and found what he was looking for in no time. He wiped perspiration from his forehead.

"I'd like a printout of this," he said. Holly nodded. As an afterthought, Modell asked her for a cup of coffee, "whenever you get the chance."

Holly hesitated before leaning over Modell to bring up the Print function on the keyboard. Modell loved this thrill. This power. He could have worked for the FBI. He was smarter than the people who did. He could have had an assistant to fetch him coffee while he busted cults, counterfeiters, serial killers. But they said he wasn't good enough. Modell knew who was going to have the last laugh. As Holly pressed the Command button to begin the printout, Modell studied the bruises on her face.

"I wish I could get my hands on the guy who did that to you, Holly," Modell said sincerely. "I'd sure make him pay."

Holly's eyes blinked rapidly. Modell reached up to touch the scratches that were still a couple of weeks away from healing completely.

Outside the office, Assistant Director Walter Skinner rounded the corner, skimming through a sheaf of papers as he walked. There was a specific name he was looking for and he hoped Ms. Patton would be able to narrow the search field to lessen the burden. The closed blinds of the office caught his eye right away. Skinner noticed details. He slowed down at the door and peered inside before entering. He heard a faint voice he didn't recognize.

"That's just fine, Holly. Now if you could—"

Skinner eased the door open and found a stranger with a pile of computer printouts in one hand, a mug of coffee in the other. Skinner quietly shut the door behind him.

"Can I help you?" he asked.

Modell was surprised by Skinner's presence, but not at all worried by him. He returned his attention to his printout sheets.

"No thanks," he said as he set down his coffee. "We're just fine."

Skinner looked from Holly back to Modell. Then he saw what Modell was reading—personnel files with background information about the agents.

"Look, I'm kinda in the middle of something," Modell added when Skinner didn't leave immediately.

Skinner grabbed the documents out of Modell's hand and backed him toward a wall away from the door.

"Who are you?" he demanded as he severely invaded Modell's personal space. "What are you doing here?"

"Take a walk, Mel Cooley," Modell spat as he tried to push Skinner.

That was a mistake. Skinner grabbed Modell by his arms, spun him, and slapped a choke hold on him in one quick motion. Coffee went flying as Skinner slammed Modell's face into the side of a file cabinet. Modell struggled, but it wasn't much of a contest. Skinner had one of his arms wrenched up behind his back. He forced Modell's chin up on top of the cabinet.

"Let me go," Modell hissed between gritted teeth. "Let me go."

Skinner lifted his arm higher to let Modell know who was in charge.

"Shut up," he commanded. "Holly, call security."

But Holly ignored him. Modell managed to jerk his head toward her.

"He's the one!" Modell barked. "He's the man who mugged you, Holly. He's hurting me."

Skinner watched, perplexed. "Holly!" he barked.

"Make him stop hurting me," Modell said.

"Shut up!" Skinner shouted. "Holly, *now!*"

She didn't move.

"Dammit," Skinner said, frustrated. He would deal with Holly later. Reaching out with one hand, he grabbed the phone and dialed a zero.

As he writhed in Skinner's grasp, a bead of

sweat rolled down Modell's temple. His bright eyes were riveted on Holly.

"Make him stop hurting me . . ." he pleaded.

Holly fumbled through her purse, grabbing madly for something. Skinner spoke into the phone.

"We've got a situation here. Fourth floor. Computer Rec—"

Before Skinner could finish his sentence, Holly withdrew a can of Mace and sprayed a jet of it directly into Skinner's face. He dropped to the floor, choking. Modell snatched up the computer printouts. As he bolted past Skinner, who had struggled to his hands and knees, Modell left instructions with Holly.

"Hurt him back," he whispered in her ear. "Hurt him back."

Modell flew out the door and was gone, leaving Holly standing over Skinner, her Mace clutched in her fingers and a look of hatred painted across her face. She saw the man who had mugged her. She remembered the humiliation she'd felt when he had punched her, then shoved her to the pavement. And here he was now, at her mercy, right in front of her. Fury rose up inside her. She began to growl. Then, with all the force her 120 pounds could muster, Holly stepped toward Skinner and kicked him in the ribs. It felt good. So she did it again. And again. She didn't stop until security arrived and dragged her away, still growling.

Chapter Ten

Holly sat in a chair surrounded by FBI agents: Scully, Skinner, and several other agents who either needed to be briefed on the breakdown in office security or were just plain curious. Holly's face was buried in her hands. Totally devastated by what she had done, she could barely speak.

"Sir," she said, her voice quavering, "I'm so terribly . . . terribly sorry. I don't know w-why I . . . Oh God."

She broke down again, sobbing into her hands. Eventually she raised her tear-filled eyes to the room.

"I'm so sorry."

Walter Skinner appraised the woman grimly. Cuts and scrapes were visible on his face, but it was his ribs that were killing him. He was able to stand, but every breath reminded him of the beating he had taken. He decided the assembled crowd had heard all they needed.

"Hit the bricks," he said, omitting any pleasantries.

All the agents cleared out quickly except for Skinner and Scully, who closed the office door for privacy. She spoke gently. "Holly, can you tell us anything more to help us understand what made you attack Assistant Director Skinner?"

Holly sniffed and wiped her face. She kept her eyes directed at the floor.

"It's like I was watching myself from across the room, doing these things . . . these . . ." As she recalled the experience, Holly became frightened anew. "It was like he was with me inside my head."

"Modell?" Scully asked.

Holly's nod was barely perceptible. Behind her, the office door quietly opened and Mulder entered.

"That's the only way I know how to put it," she said.

Scully watched the woman intently, trying to understand. Deputy Kerber, Agent Collins, Holly—Mulder's theory, his talk of mind control, was starting to seem like the only viable explanation. Scully just wished she knew how it worked.

Mulder waited a moment before addressing Skinner.

"Sir, can I have a word with you outside?"

Skinner nodded. Scully put a comforting hand on Holly's shoulder before leaving the weeping woman alone in the office. She joined Mulder and Skinner in the hallway. Mulder spoke quietly.

"I reviewed the building security tapes. Modell can be seen entering and leaving unnoticed. He had the word 'pass' on his lapel. Guards who waved him by don't remember seeing him at all."

Skinner wasn't sure what Mulder's point was.

"And you're saying this same mysterious

phenomenon is the reason I have heel marks on my face?"

Mulder nodded. Skinner turned to Scully for her opinion.

"I have to agree with Agent Mulder," she said, though somewhat reluctantly. "Sir, I can't begin to explain how, but Modell is responsible for your injuries."

Scully's sober assessment carried weight with Skinner. He dropped the subject and moved on to other business. He turned to Mulder.

"Why is this guy interested in you?"

Mulder hadn't realized he was.

"What do you mean?"

"He left here with only one file: yours," Skinner said. "He didn't access any others."

Mulder was at a loss for an answer. He shook his head. Scully glanced at her partner, concerned.

"Now he knows where you live," she said.

Skinner chose to look at the positives. "And you know where *he* lives. Go pick him up."

"For what?" Mulder asked. "Criminal tres-
pass? That's all we can get him on now."

The plan didn't satisfy Mulder. He remembered what had happened the last time they'd
had Modell in custody. He wasn't sure they
could avoid the same thing this time, though
at least they'd have evidence on videotape.

Skinner looked at Scully and Mulder. The
thought of a killer having the personnel file of
any of his agents chilled him.

"It's enough for a warrant," he said. He left
before either had time to argue.

Chapter Eleven

The federal SWAT cops announced their presence at the same instant they battered down Modell's front door.

"Raid! Federal officers!" they screamed as they swarmed into the apartment. They leveled their assault rifles, mounted with a thin red laser that cut through the darkness. Each officer wore full riot gear: helmet, goggles, bulletproof vest. Mulder and Scully had instructed them to stay in pairs. They didn't want Modell in a room alone with any officers this time.

Within a second, a dozen officers were searching rooms, covering each other as they threw open doors and pointed their rifles into the darkest corners. Agent Burst followed the men, scowling. He wanted Pusher in a bad way.

"Modell!" he shouted, daring him to show his face.

Mulder and Scully were last through the door, a bit less adrenalized than their fellow agent. Scully felt along the walls until she found the light switches. She called to the others, "Lights coming on."

She and Mulder entered a large, spartan living room. Aside from a bag of golf clubs in the corner, the room was devoid of any personal effects that would give it a modicum of individuality. Mulder and Scully holstered their guns and glanced around. A small TV set and VCR sat in the corner. On the screen, a young John Barrymore, his eyes glowing, was mesmerizing Marian Marsh. The sound was turned low, but Scully could hear the rhythmic cadence of Barrymore's words. She turned and saw Mulder staring at the set as well.

"*Svengali*," she said, happy to beat Mulder on a point of cultural literacy. She'd seen the melodrama about the obsessed hypnotist on American Movie Classics.

Mulder nodded. He wasn't amused by Modell's sense of humor. He had left the tape playing intentionally. That meant Modell had known they'd be coming for him. Mulder pulled out the self-adhesive search warrant and slapped it over John Barrymore's eyes.

Burst and the lead SWAT cop, a Lieutenant Brophy, converged back on the living room from opposite ends of the apartment.

"All clear. No one home," said Brophy.

"Search the whole building," Burst ordered.

"Nearby buildings, too," Scully added. "We know Modell likes to watch from a distance."

Agent Burst nodded at the SWAT team, who began carrying out their new orders immediately. Burst holstered his pistol and glanced around impatiently. Next to him, Mulder and Scully pulled on their exam gloves.

"Check the place out. I'll go talk to the neighbors," Burst said. He was happy to let the other agents sift through clues. He was still more interested in finding Modell.

Scully clicked off the television set as Burst exited. She began to rummage through the living room while Mulder drifted into the kitchen. He opened the refrigerator. Along with three oranges, a bottle of ketchup, and a box of Arm & Hammer baking soda was a huge stockpile of CarboBoost High Energy Protein Drink. The cans filled three shelves. Mulder called to Scully.

"Check this out."

Scully entered the kitchen and peered into the refrigerator. She frowned, not understanding what sort of clue this might be. Mulder's eyes narrowed. He reached in and pulled out a can.

"Mango-Kiwi Tropical Swirl," he said solemnly. "Now I know we're dealing with a madman."

Scully smiled before returning to the living room. Mulder closed the fridge and began rifling through the drawers. Fifteen minutes later Modell's belongings were in disarray. Mulder had gone through the kitchen with a fine-tooth comb. Now he was working on the bedroom. He stopped in front of a '70s-era rattan bookcase that had plenty of room for the dozen or so books that were propped up inside it. Mulder began perusing the titles: Eastern philosophy, martial arts, Bushido, Zen. Mulder came to a big volume about the human brain. He pulled it down and plopped it onto the bed. He picked up the next book on the shelf—also about the brain. This one he began reading.

Scully, in the meantime, was searching the bathroom and wrapping up a call on her cell phone. She stood by the open medicine cabinet, studying a prescription bottle in her hand.

"Right," she said into the phone. "Thank you very much."

Mulder appeared in the bathroom doorway. Scully tucked away her phone and presented him with the prescription bottle she'd been holding.

"Tegretol," she said.

Mulder held the bottle up to the light.

"What's it for?"

"It's to relieve Modell's seizures. He has temporal-lobe epilepsy. I just talked to his doctor's office. They wouldn't give me much over the phone." Scully paused. She thought Mulder would find the next bit of information significant. "Just that the prescription dates back to April 1994."

Scully watched Mulder's reaction. She took some amount of pleasure in how well she could read her stoic partner's expressions in certain situations. Right now, she swore she could practically see the gears in his mind whirring.

"What causes epilepsy that late in life?"

"Head injury," Scully replied. "Neurological disease. A brain tumor or lesion . . . "

Mulder heard what he was expecting. He began nodding before he broke in to speak.

"A tumor? Scully, the growth of brain tumors has been linked with instances of psychic ability."

Scully had seen the reports Mulder was citing.

"Mulder, those reports are completely unsubstanti—"

"Just bear with me," Mulder said, cutting her off. "What if this suggestive power of Modell's is actually a form of psychokinesis?"

Scully considered the suggestion. "Brought on by a brain tumor?"

"It fits," Mulder said, making his case almost as it occurred to him. "All those protein shakes in the fridge—why does he need them? What if it's to replace the metabolic energy he burns in the process of controlling someone's will?"

Scully admired the way Mulder assimilated new clues and pieced them into a theory, but she felt part of her job was to voice new questions that Mulder's theories elicited.

"Mulder, if Modell was suffering from a brain tumor, would he be well enough to play these cat-and-mouse games with us?"

"Maybe he's not," Mulder replied. "Maybe that's the whole point."

"What do you mean?"

"His exhaustion at the driving range—it

looked like he was *letting* us capture him. But what if he was too wiped out to escape? Too sick? And why would such a proficient killer confess to murders he had already gotten away with?"

As he said it, an explanation came to Mulder.

"What if he's dying?" he asked.

Scully saw where Mulder was heading. She spoke quietly, intrigued by his logic.

"And he wants to go out in a blaze of glory?" she added, furthering his case.

"Not with a whimper but a bang."

Chapter Twelve

The phone in Modell's living room began to ring. Mulder looked at Scully. If Modell was the caller, it would put an exclamation point on his hypothesis. Scully took the bottle of Tegretol back from Mulder as they walked into the other room. The phone, sitting atop a small dining table next to the sofa, rang again. Agent Burst put his hand on the receiver and glanced around the room to make sure everyone was ready. The SWAT cops who had been searching nearby buildings began streaming back into Modell's living room.

"Get the tracer gear," Burst ordered.

One of the cops tore back out the door and down the stairs. Unhappy that they weren't prepared for this possibility, Burst answered the phone as it began its fourth ring.

"Hello," he said.

"Hey, hey, hey! Whaddya say?" came the voice on the other end.

Burst nodded to Scully and Mulder—it was Modell. The partners walked quickly to the phone in the bedroom. They could hear Burst's response as they moved through the apartment. The agent attempted to match the odd satirical cheeriness of Modell's voice.

"What's up, Modell? How're you doin'? Long time no see. Told you I knew where you lived."

Scully lifted the receiver quietly. Mulder leaned in so they could both hear the conversation taking place. Burst was still speaking when they picked up.

"Apartment's nice. Who's your decorator, Modell? The Grinch that stole Christmas?"

"Hah," Modell said, faking a laugh at Burst's joke. "This must be Agent Frank Burst, the guy with the great name. Frank, are Agents Mulder and Scully there? They listening?"

Modell waited a moment for a reply. When none came, he continued in his odd tone. "I've got two phones," he said. Mulder thought Modell sounded exuberant . . . almost joyful.

Scully thought the voice sounded modulated, like the first night they'd talked to him on the pay phone. She realized it was probably being filtered through several low-tech, yet effective, scrambling devices. Mulder made the decision to speak.

"We're here," he said into the phone.

"Perfect," Modell chirped. Then he took a deep breath. "Frank, how much do you weigh?"

In the living room the SWAT cop arrived with the steel suitcase that housed the tracing gear. He set it down on the coffee table in front of Lieutenant Brophy. Brophy took off his gloves and began adjusting the frequency as another SWAT cop expertly cut into the line running to the phone. Burst watched the pair working beside him. He stalled.

"Excuse me?"

The lieutenant nodded at Burst. They were set up.

"About how much do you weigh?" Modell repeated.

The lieutenant mouthed "Keep him on."

Burst had no idea why Modell was curious about his size. He didn't really care. He put his hand over the receiver.

"Anything to keep you talking, you worthless piece of . . ." The lieutenant grinned up at his superior. The first numbers of the area code appeared on the screen of the tracing unit. Burst removed his hand and allowed Modell to hear him.

"I don't know. One-ninety. One-ninety-five."

"Hah! Two-fifteen if you're an ounce. You're totally the wrong weight for your height. I mean—no offense—but you're built like a fireplug."

Burst watched as another number appeared on the screen. They were getting closer.

"Yeah," he said to Modell, "and I got stubby little legs that are gonna kick you right in the ass. Is this actually going somewhere, Modell?"

In the bedroom, Scully was considering Mulder's theory. Maybe this *was* Modell's dying wish: to be caught. To play the game close to the edge.

Modell answered Burst's question. "Just that it can't be healthy. And you look like maybe you're a smoker. You probably take a little drink now and then, eat greasy fried foods. Sausage and bacon, eggs over easy—"

"Frank," Mulder cut in. He had a bad feeling about the conversation.

Modell continued. "—onion rings that soak those dark stains through the cardboard. And I'm guessing you work that salt shaker like a maraca."

Mulder definitely didn't like where this was heading. "Frank. *Frank!* Hang up!" he said through the bedroom extension.

But Burst ignored Mulder, even though he was beginning to tremble, beads of perspiration were forming on his forehead, and for some reason he couldn't keep from grinding his teeth. Burst had his eyes fixed on the tracing unit. In the past few seconds, Brophy had locked in on two more digits. Burst wanted this guy bad. He'd seen one cop die and another set himself on fire. He was going to hold on to that phone for as long as it took.

"What're you talking about, Modell?" he asked. "What's your point?"

"You know what that's doing to your arteries?" Modell intoned. "Terrible things."

That was enough for Mulder. Alarm bells were going off in his head. He left Scully in the bedroom holding the phone and bolted into the living room. On the phone, Modell continued. Continued pushing.

"Waxy yellow chunks of plaque are tumbling through your bloodstream . . ."

Burst was breathing faster. Sweat was pouring from him.

" . . . sticking like glue to your arterial walls . . . squeezing your aorta shut. Can you feel it? Can you feel it squeeze?"

Mulder shouldered past the SWAT team. Burst tried to turn his back on him, but Mulder got right up in his face.

"Hang up the phone, Frank," he pleaded.

"Come on, man, hang *up*."

Burst watched as another digit locked in on the liquid crystal display of the tracing unit. "Back off!" he screamed at Mulder.

Mulder had lost his patience. It was his turn to scream.

"I said *hang up the phone!*"

"*I said back off!*" Burst shouted back.

In the background, Modell's voice continued.

"Ever hear of pachyemia, Frank? It's when the blood thickens up in your veins like strawberry jam."

Mulder reached over to thunk down the button that would disconnect the call, but Burst slapped his hand away. Two burly SWAT cops muscled Mulder back against the wall. Burst barked orders to the lieutenant through clenched teeth. "Finish the trace!"

Mulder made another attempt to get to the phone. This time the SWAT cops shoved him hard against the wall. Another number appeared on the tracing unit. Burst wouldn't have to keep Pusher on much longer.

In the bedroom Scully was aware of the commotion. She didn't want to leave the receiver. She thought either she or Mulder ought to keep monitoring the call, searching for clues, but she recognized the sound of a body getting thrown against a wall. She hung up her phone and moved into the living room.

"Mulder?" she called before seeing him pinned up against the wall. Three SWAT cops were now holding him back. Mulder was hoping anyone would listen to him.

"Hang up the phone!" he shouted.

Scully glanced over at Burst. Her medical training told her right away that this man was having a heart attack. His face was beet red. He was sweating profusely. His gasping indicated he wasn't getting enough oxygen. Scully saw the line leading away from the phone. She followed it with her eyes to a jack against the far wall. On impulse she darted for it, but another SWAT cop was on her before she made it. He yanked her away and kept his body between her and her goal.

Mulder kept pleading with Burst, shouting "Hang up!" over and over. But Burst had only two numbers to go, and besides that, he couldn't hang up now if he wanted to.

"Your heart flatlines," Modell droned. "Beeeeeeeeeeeeeeeep."

Burst's head jerked up from the phone. He stared at Mulder, then Scully, a sudden, terrible resignation etched on his face. His eyes went glassy. He let out a slow breath and dropped the receiver as he collapsed to the floor. The phone fell beside him. No one knew if he even heard Pusher's final words.

"You die, Frank."

The SWAT cops stared, too amazed to really comprehend what had just happened. Scully pushed her way through to get to Burst. She knelt beside the body and began to check his vital signs. From the phone on the floor next to her, she could hear Modell. He was cheery once more.

"Frank?" came the voice.

Mulder had broken through the barricade of stunned cops himself. He too kneeled beside Burst. He too detected the glee in Modell's voice as it emerged from the phone's receiver.

"Yo, Frankie!"

Mulder and Scully locked eyes. Scully had her fingers pressed to Burst's neck.

"No pulse."

She snapped at one of the cops who appeared to be doing nothing, "We're going to need an ambulance."

The cop was on his cell phone in an instant, providing the address for a dispatcher. Scully leaned over Burst's body and began pumping his sternum with her palm. She counted as she pumped.

"One thousand one. One thousand two. One thousand three. One thousand four. One thousand five."

After the count of five, Scully leaned over Burst's face and administered mouth-to-mouth resuscitation. By the time she came up for air, she'd lost patience with the spectators surrounding her.

"Who's helping me here?" she demanded.

One of the SWAT cops dropped to his knees and took over on Burst's rib cage. The two continued the synchronized procedure.

Mulder lifted the phone receiver from the floor to his ear.

"Modell?"

"Hey, Mulder. How's Frankie Boy?" came the reply.

Mulder forced himself to keep his anger in check. The tracer operator sat back down in front of his equipment. Mulder glanced at Scully, who was holding two fingers to Burst's carotid artery. She was sweating from her effort. She looked up at Mulder and shook her head grimly. Mulder paused before returning his attention to the phone. He spoke quietly.

"What is it, really, that you want, Modell?"

"A worthy adversary," answered the voice. "It's obviously not that fat lump lying at your feet." Modell paused. Mulder's silence confirmed for Pusher what he already assumed was true. "Now I'm hoping it's you."

"Why me?" Mulder answered dubiously.

"I've read all about you," Modell responded. "You're a top criminal profiler. Oxford University grad. All-around bright young man. You know what makes guys like me tick, right? You think you see right through old Bob Modell."

Mulder watched as Scully continued her futile efforts to revive Burst.

"*Sick* old Bob Modell," said Mulder. "Are you dying, Bob? Did you want to take some innocent people with you?"

This time the beat of silence confirmed information for Mulder. For once, Mulder thought, he and Scully knew something before Modell wanted them to. Eventually Modell recovered.

"Biology tells us we're all dying," he said, "and original sin tells me ain't nobody innocent."

Mulder watched as Scully gave up on Burst. She stood and shook her head again. The man was dead. The lieutenant assigned to the tracing unit was having trouble concentrating on his task. He couldn't believe what had happened right in front of him.

"Some are less innocent than others," Mulder said to Modell. "Why don't you tell me where you are?"

"What? You want the phone number?" Modell asked in a why-didn't-you-say-so tone. "Um, sure. 555-0197." Modell even allowed time for the number to be jotted down. "It's just a pay phone. In two minutes I'll be long gone."

Mulder leaned back and watched as the final number appeared on the tracing unit. It matched the number Modell had given him. Mulder knew at that moment that Burst's death had been in vain. Mulder had to fight to keep swallowing. He felt like he was going to be sick. Standing above him, Scully watched carefully. She was going to shoot the damn phone jack if even one bead of sweat appeared on Mulder's face.

"You mean you killed him for nothing, you sick bastard?"

Modell only seemed happy at that conclusion. "Me? Haven't you caught on, Mulder?" he taunted. "They all kill *themselves*."

With that, the line clicked dead. Mulder hung up and looked to Scully.

"You all right?" she asked.

Mulder nodded. Beside him the angry young lieutenant yanked off his headphones and exhaled. The rest of the SWAT team stood quietly around Agent Burst's body. The air of defeat in the room was palpable.

"Where was Modell calling from?" asked Mulder.

Lieutenant Brophy clicked a few more buttons on his equipment before answering.

"A gas station parking lot. Twelve thousand block of Chain Bridge Road." The lieutenant shook his head. "It's a pay phone, just like he said."

Mulder stepped over to view the Fairfax County map on the tracer's screen. His finger found the gas station, then slid up a few centimeters to a highlighted location just up the road from it. Mulder squinted.

"Fairfax Mercy Hospital," he said, indicating the spot to Scully. "Right up the street from there."

"Fairfax Mercy . . . " Scully repeated in a whisper. She knew that had meaning. She reached into her jacket pocket and found her answer.

"Fairfax Mercy Pharmacy," she said as she held up the bottle of Tegretol. She read off the label. " 'Fairfax Mercy Pharmacy'. He must need regular treatment."

Mulder pulled out his cell phone and dialed Information.

"Let's find out," he said.

As the phone began to ring, Mulder heard the siren of the ambulance coming for Frank Burst.

Chapter Thirteen

During the morning hours, cars continued to enter and exit Fairfax Mercy Hospital, oblivious to the precise quasi-military operation taking place around them. SWAT snipers had already taken position behind an air compressor on the roof of a neighboring parking garage.

A member of the SWAT team trained his weapon on the back tire of a nondescript Chevrolet moving slowly through the parking lot, then shifted his scope to the front entrance of the hospital pharmacy. He eased the bolt on his rifle forward, listening for the tiny oiled click that let him know it was in place.

On the ground below him, another sniper

hunkered down, his body as still as granite. He awaited radio instructions before moving his squad into position. When he received the All Clear in his headphones, he motioned for three more agents to advance and, momentarily, take the lead position.

On the other side of the medical complex, families of patients strolled through a parking lot without noticing the dozen cops moving from car to car like ghosts. After every third vehicle, one of the cops would stay behind, thinning their ranks but creating a net that wouldn't allow Pusher to escape or start an impromptu tête-à-tête chat with any of the team members. One of the cops stayed behind when he reached a tan Cadillac. He had already memorized the license plate of this car. It was Modell's, the same one in which he'd been arrested by Mulder. The SWAT man pulled his right glove off with his teeth and felt the hood. He nodded to the cop stationed thirty yards in front of him. That cop signaled to another who would have been undetectable had his squadmate not known where to look. The third cop pulled his headset microphone down in front of his mouth.

"We found Modell's car. Engine's still warm. He's probably in the building."

In the unmarked black SWAT van parked in the service entrance behind a row of dumpsters that hid it from view, Scully and Mulder heard the message.

Mulder and Lieutenant Brophy stood by the radio console in the back of the cramped surveillance van. Scully moved as far away as possible within the windowless confines of the van and listened as a hospital administrator fed her information concerning the whereabouts of one Robert Modell. A dozen television monitors inside the van displayed color bars. Normal procedure would have called for tapping in to the hospital's closed-circuit system. But today there simply hadn't been enough time. A reel-to-reel tape deck silently recorded the radio chatter of the operation.

A second voice came over the radio. It was the other unit leader.

"All entrances covered. Do we hold or go in?"

Mulder stretched his neck. There wasn't a response to that question that sounded good to him. The lieutenant awaited his order.

"Hold," said Mulder without much conviction.

Lieutenant Brophy repeated the order into the microphone on the radio console. Scully thanked the woman she'd been talking to and punched the End button on her cell phone. She checked her watch before speaking.

"The outpatient office says Modell is scheduled for a 9:30 MRI. That's now."

The lieutenant listened. He felt he was the only one in the van vaguely aware of the fact that two dozen highly trained SWAT men were currently in position and anxious to drag a cop killer out of the building.

"How do you want to play this?" he asked.

Mulder and Scully looked to each other for an answer. Neither was sure how to contain

Modell, how to withstand his powers, or how to prevent him from using them. Eventually Mulder spoke.

"I think I should go in alone."

"Why?" Scully responded.

It sounded to her as though Mulder was taking an unnecessary risk. Brophy didn't like the idea much better.

"My team can flush him out," he suggested.

Mulder remained blank-faced. "What if Modell turns one of your men against the others? In a crowded hospital?" he asked. The lieutenant glanced away. He hadn't considered that. Mulder pressed on. "Let's give him what he wants."

Scully knew exactly what that meant.

"You," she said.

Scully studied Mulder for a moment. He looked nervous, maybe even a little scared. *Good,* she thought. *That fear might be what keeps him alive.*

Mulder was still justifying the plan. In his

own way, he was looking for an alternative, but he saw none.

"If we're separated," he told Scully, "we stand a better chance. I'll go in miked. That way you'll know where he is and what he's doing."

Mulder turned his attention to the lieutenant. "Give me a radio—something so I can keep my hands free."

Brophy opened an equipment locker and reached inside. "I've got just what you need," he said.

He yanked a lunch-box-size metal case out of the locker and set it down on the countertop. Its contents were marked on the lid: EYES AND EARS. The lieutenant opened the lid, revealing a featherweight apparatus that provided both video and audio transmission.

Before Lieutenant Brophy began hooking Mulder up, he asked him to put on a bulletproof vest. While Mulder did that, the lieutenant ordered the SWAT team members to hold their positions. He didn't envy them.

Holding a position while maintaining a constant guard was one of the most difficult disciplines a SWAT cop had to master.

Lieutenant Brophy worked quickly but not frantically. He placed the headset on Mulder, then clipped the transmitter to the back of his vest. An earphone plugged in to Mulder's left ear allowed him to use his right to listen to ambient sound. The microphone was stuck to Mulder's throat with an adhesive patch. An amazingly tiny video camera jutted out from the earpiece and lined up parallel to his eyes. The lieutenant briefed Mulder on the equipment as he adjusted the microphone level.

"Two lux video camera—it'll practically see in the dark. It's designed for bomb disposal to keep only one officer at risk."

Mulder and Scully turned to look at a small video monitor built in to the van's communications console. Every time Mulder moved his head, the monitor reflected his field of vision.

"Think I get the Playboy Channel?"

The lieutenant chuckled. Scully rolled her eyes.

"Smile, Scully . . ." Mulder said.

Mulder regarded his partner. She couldn't even return his stare. He reluctantly unfastened his holstered pistol and presented it to her. The decision surprised her.

"Take it," Scully urged.

Mulder bent low in front of where his partner was sitting and pushed the weapon into her hands. He spoke quietly.

"I wouldn't want to find myself pointing this at anyone but Modell."

The move went against Scully's better judgment, but she complied. She took one hand out from under the gun and placed it on top of Mulder's hands. He forced a smile.

"Let's get this show on the road," he said.

Chapter Fourteen

The sliding-glass double doors of the emergency room whooshed open on Mulder's approach. He entered the ER looking like a cyborg sentry on his day off—the video camera headset combined with the bullet-proof vest caused orderlies and patients to stop suddenly and stare. Mulder knew where he was going, and he moved briskly through the reception area. A nurse stood as if she were going to question him, but he flashed his badge as he approached.

"Federal agent," he said. "Go about your business as usual."

The nurse let him by.

Mulder walked down a corridor, past a sign that read MAGNETIC RESONANCE IMAGING. The arrow on the sign confirmed that he was heading the correct way. He spoke quietly, as if to himself.

"Scully, you reading me?"

Inside the SWAT van Scully was watching Mulder's progress on the video monitor. She took note of the signs on the walls as well as the operating rooms he passed. The faces of gawking nurses and orderlies glided past, in, then out of, view. Scully knew she and Mulder weren't exactly working with a strategy that hinged on surprise, but the conspicuousness of her partner still made her nervous.

"I'm reading you, Mulder."

So was the lieutenant. Both he and Scully were wearing headsets so they could listen to Mulder as well as any of the other SWAT cops. As he proceeded down the hall, Mulder continued to mark his progress.

"Nothing out of the ordinary," he reported.

The lieutenant flipped a switch that allowed him to address his team.

"SWAT team: Hold outside," he ordered.

A voice came back over the headset.

"SWAT team still holding."

As Scully and the lieutenant continued to monitor Mulder's video transmission, they saw him peer into rooms on either side of the hallway, occasionally startling the occupants.

Suddenly, the sound of a gunshot threatened to tear a hole through the speaker cones.

"Mulder?" Scully checked anxiously.

Another shot echoed through the building.

The view on the screen indicated that Mulder was running toward the danger. Frightened doctors came flying at the camera, running away from the sound of gunfire.

"Two shots fired," Mulder reported.

The lieutenant spoke into the microphone. "SWAT team: Move into—"

"No!" Mulder interjected. "Keep the SWAT team *out*. Just wait a minute. Let me see what the hell's going on."

Mulder tried to calm the panicked hospital employees who were fleeing the intensive-care unit.

"Everyone continue moving," he shouted. "Federal agent . . . keep on going . . . clear everybody out."

Mulder turned his attention back to Scully.

"Can you see what's going on here?"

As Mulder swam against the current of people, white static began blotting out the video image. All Scully was receiving were distant yells and the hard breathing of Mulder, who was running.

"Wait! We're losing you," Scully called.

The lieutenant tried as well. "Mulder! Agent Mulder!"

But nothing came back over the screen except static. Scully headed for the door. As she did so, the image fluttered, faded back to static, then cleared again.

"Wait," called the lieutenant. "Agent Scully!"

"You getting this back there?" Mulder asked.

A black-and-white image on the video monitor showed a view of the MRI suite. Two bodies were sprawled out on the floor. Thin trickles of blood seeped from their heads. Scully sat back down at the console, her eyes glued to the monitor.

"What happened, Mulder?" she asked.

The sound of an artificial lung mechanically pumping away unnerved Mulder as he examined the bodies, checking the pulse of each and confirming that each was in fact dead. The first one appeared to be an MRI technician. He was wearing a white lab coat and he lay a few feet from his operator's console. Mulder had seen enough crime scenes to know the technician had been sitting in his chair when he'd been shot. It was the force of the bullet that had blown him back the several feet to where he now lay. A few feet away, a hospital security guard was sprawled facedown. Mulder reflexively searched for evidence. He noticed five .357-caliber rounds nearby—two fired and three unfired.

"I think the guard shot the technician, then himself," Mulder said as he glanced around. His eyes as well as the video camera came to rest on the guard's empty holster. "His gun is missing. Lieutenant Brophy, tell your men Modell could be headed their way."

The lieutenant got on the radio. "SWAT team: Suspect is armed and is possibly making his way out of the building."

"We copy. We're ready for him," came the immediate response of the squad leader positioned in front of the hospital.

The squad leader in the back answered nearly as quickly.

"Shooters in position."

With the background voices fresh in his ears, Mulder continued his search of the room. In front of him a computer monitor rested on the MRI control station. The station butted against a glass partition. On the other side of the partition, he saw the MRI table. Beyond that—

"Wait, wait, wait," came Scully's voice into Mulder's ear. "Mulder, take a closer look at that computer screen."

"Over here?" asked Mulder as he drew nearer the station.

"Yeah, yeah, yeah. Right there."

Mulder realized that what he was looking at on the screen was a three-dimensional image of a human brain. Even to Mulder's untrained eye a dark spot was visible inside the brain. Mulder scanned the top of the screen and came to a patient's name: MODELL, ROBERT P.

Inside the van, Scully leaned closer to the video image, studying it.

"There . . ." she said. "That mass in the temporal lobe. You were right."

Mulder used his finger to point to the dark spot on the screen.

"This? The tumor?"

"Yes," Scully responded. "Check in front of you. Modell's chart should be there."

Mulder found the clipboard on top of a stack next to the monitor. He leafed through the pages, nodding as he read.

"We're batting a thousand, Scully. He's dying. He has nothing to lose."

Scully didn't like the odds of dealing with a killer who had nothing to lose. Those were the killers who took everyone out with them, then put the gun to their own head. There was nothing they were willing to negotiate. Nothing had meaning to them.

"Mulder," she said. "Get out of there."

Mulder heard Scully's voice, but he didn't respond. He was trying to keep perfectly still. He had heard something else in the room. Something that didn't belong. In the van, both Scully and the lieutenant were struck by how still the camera was held in place. It made Scully antsy. She could almost sense Mulder's fear.

"Mulder!" she said again, louder and with more conviction.

The monitor indicated that Mulder was remaining motionless. In the MRI room, Mulder strained his ears. There it was again. From behind him. Mulder spun.

Out in the van, the lieutenant and Scully watched as the camera panned hard to the left. The room whipped by in a black-and-white blur. The camera settled on the distorted face of a smirking Robert Modell.

Scully could make out the large satin-nickel Colt Python pointed directly at Mulder's head. The camera attempted to adjust its autofocus, but before it could, Scully saw Modell's hand reach up toward Mulder's head.

White static filled the screen of the TV monitor.

Scully bolted from her chair, terror filling her face. For all she knew, Mulder might already be dead.

Chapter Fifteen

Scully pulled on a bulletproof vest as she raced through the corridors of the hospital, passing four itchy SWAT cops in position along the wall. She reached the corner of the hallway, but she didn't peer around it. Lieutenant Brophy waited there for her while one of the other cops looked around the corner with a mirror mounted onto a boom pole. The lieutenant laid out the situation as he knew it.

"We think they're three doors down. We've got both ends sewn up tight, but there's six critical-care rooms we can't get to. If we gas the hall we might kill those patients."

Scully took in the information and nodded. Like her partner before her, Scully reluctantly unclipped her holster and handed it to the lieutenant. He took it from her, then spoke in quiet wonder.

"Why do we keep giving this guy exactly what he wants?"

Scully didn't have an answer. She only knew she couldn't be trusted with Modell and a gun. Nobody could.

"Just wait for a signal from me," she told the lieutenant. She didn't bother trying to answer his question. The lieutenant lowered his goggles and prepared for a battle he hoped would never happen. Scully looked to the cop holding the mirror.

"All clear," he said.

Scared to numbness, but resolute, Scully took tentative steps into the hall. She felt for all the world like a hydrophobe wading out into the ocean just waiting for something to drag her under. Scully glanced back at the corner she'd just come from and was surprised to see that she'd only put four or five yards between her and the cavalry. She couldn't see the men, but she could see the mirror peering out around the corner. Scully slowly eased past the open doors of two critical-care rooms that faced each other on either side of the hallway. Inside the rooms, unconscious patients breathed raspily with the aid of ventilators. She pictured the charred body of Agent Collins recuperating in a room like this. Scully wondered how she would be leaving the hospital.

Scully kept easing forward toward the third door. All remained quiet in the hallway except for the faint mechanical clicking of various life-support machines. When she arrived at her destination, she kept her body behind the wall and away from the entrance. She reached out and pushed the door with her right hand. As it opened slightly, she could see two more critical-care patients lying unconscious in their beds. She pushed the door further and saw her partner stripped down to his T-shirt and slacks, sitting at a round table.

"Mulder?" she called.

But he didn't respond. He kept looking at something directly across from him. Scully pushed the door completely open. The some-thing that Mulder had been looking at was Modell. Between them, on the table, rested the Colt. Currently it was pointing at Mulder. Modell was dressed in teal doctor's scrubs. Scully noted his condition. Pasty. Wrung out. Slick with sweat. The way he'd looked the day they picked him up at the driving range. Scully spotted Mulder's vest and headset lying on a heap on the floor. She didn't know yet whether he had removed them at gun-point or whether Modell had Mulder in what her partner had once referred to as "the whammy."

Modell didn't lift his gaze from Mulder when he spoke.

"Thanks for joining us," he said flatly.

Scully tried a tactic that she knew to be a long shot.

"We've got a dozen law enforcement offi-cers right outside this room. Another thirty in the parking lot."

"It's a regular convention," Modell re-sponded.

Scully didn't let the killer's flippancy deter her. "So whatever you've got planned, it's not going to work out the way you want it to."

"You don't know what I got planned," Modell muttered, his voice low and menacing.

Scully thought Modell sounded as though he were having to labor physically. It was almost as if he were rationing words, conserving his energy. He wouldn't take his eyes off Mulder. Mulder seemed to be under Modell's spell. He hadn't said a thing, hadn't even looked at her since she entered the room. Scully eyed the empty chair at the table. She hesitated, then glanced back down at the gun. Modell's hand was now resting on it. Scully slowly lowered herself into the chair. She studied Mulder. Not only was he staring at Modell, Scully hadn't seen him blink.

Modell picked the gun off the table.

"Two equally skilled combatants fight to the death," he said as he popped out the cylinder. Scully remembered the five shells on the floor that she'd seen on the monitor. That meant there was one bullet left.

"One is a student of Japanese Budo—the Way of War."

Modell gave the cylinder a long spin and clicked it back into place as he spoke.

"Budo teaches the warrior to leave himself outside the battle. In other words, to disregard his own death."

Modell plunked the gun back down onto the table. Scully noted how Mulder seemed riveted by every word coming out of Modell's mouth. Mulder didn't even seem to notice the gun, he was so focused on Modell's eyes.

"Because of that," Modell continued, "the Budo warrior always wins."

Modell allowed himself a smile as he slid the gun across the table to Mulder.

"I am that warrior, and I don't fear my death. So I'll give you one pull of the trigger against me. That's a one-in-six chance."

Modell removed his hand from the top of the gun, allowing Mulder to take it. As Mulder reached for it, though, Modell prevented him momentarily by grabbing his hands.

"That's *one* pull," he reemphasized.

Then Modell let go and allowed Mulder to pick up the gun. He lifted it cautiously and pointed it at Modell.

The voice in Mulder's head told him to pull the trigger, but it was a stranger's voice—not his own. Mulder had the drop on Pusher, but his only desire was to drag him out to the SWAT cops, cuff him, read him rights. He didn't want to shoot him in cold blood. So why couldn't he just turn away?

There had been points, moments in time—when Scully opened the door or just before Modell grabbed his hands—that Mulder thought he was on the verge of winning, of reclaiming his own mind. But right now Modell was still in charge. Mulder fought it, but he could feel his finger taking up the slack on the trigger. He heard Scully's voice. He knew she was in the room, but he couldn't take his eyes off Modell.

"Wait, Mulder. Look!"

Mulder wanted to, but he couldn't.

"There's pure oxygen in this room," she said. "There's no telling what could happen if you pull that trigger."

The hammer snapped down before Scully even finished her sentence. She nearly jumped out of her seat. Modell flinched and continued to blink rapidly, but the chamber was empty. He was still alive.

Mulder knew what would come next, and it would be a nightmare. Now he desperately wanted to keep firing, to pull the trigger until he found a chamber that wasn't empty. Instead, he lowered his arm slowly and let the pistol come to rest on the slick surface of the table.

"Whew," Modell said facetiously. "Piece of cake, right?"

He gestured toward Mulder.

"Your turn."

Scully knew what Modell meant by that. "Mulder, no."

Modell topped Scully's volume.

"Mulder, *yes*. Do it!"

Mulder gave no indication that he was

hearing either of them. Inside his head a full-scale war was being waged. Mulder was using all of his will to keep himself from picking that gun back up. Modell's face was sweating like a glass of iced tea on a warm day. That was good. Mulder had to hold on longer, fight him at every turn. He wasn't just trying to keep from reaching for the gun. Mulder was sending messages to his feet to run, to his mouth to yell at Scully to get out of the room, to his eyes to tell them to look away . . .

Modell leaned in closer. His eyes bore through Mulder, concentrating utterly on him.

"Go!" he ordered.

It wasn't so much the force of the word as the fresh wave of willpower crashing into Mulder's mind . . .

Scully leaned closer to her partner. She eased a hand toward the gun and spoke gently to him. "Give that to me, Mulder. We can stop this thing right now. You and I can just walk out of this room."

Scully thought she was winning. Mulder

wasn't stopping her. Modell wasn't stopping her. She hoped that somewhere her voice was reaching into Mulder's will, helping to harden it against Modell's influence.

Before she knew what was happening, Mulder, in one swift motion, reached for the gun, lifted it, grimaced, pointed it at his own temple, and without a moment's hesitation, pulled the trigger.

The only sounds were a click and Scully screaming.

"No!"

Scully was thunderstruck. She fell back into her chair, knowing she could just as easily have been wearing the scrambled remains of Mulder's head. She was back up in an instant, shouting at Modell. "Damn you! You bastard!"

She turned to her partner. "Mulder, give me the gun."

She grabbed for the weapon that was resting again on the table, but Mulder picked it up before she could get to it. And there was a second . . . a sweet second . . . that Mulder was able to level the gun at Modell. He was so close to breaking free. Modell was using up so much energy Mulder had even seen a split second of panic in his eye, but now Modell was smiling like the cat that ate the canary. Back in control and—without even speaking this time—forcing Mulder to do something even more horrifying.

Mulder swiveled and pointed the gun at Scully's head.

He nearly choked out her name. Then he watched himself begin to pull back on the trigger.

Scully couldn't believe what was happening. She read the pain in her partner's eyes.

"Mulder! Don't do this! You're stronger than this!"

"It's your turn, Agent Scully," Modell said excitedly. He was grinning. Loving every minute.

Then he directed his stare back at Mulder. "Pull the trigger, Mulder."

Scully watched her partner. Her vest was

going to do her no good. He was aiming between her eyes. Scully had seen Mulder countless times at the firing range. He wouldn't miss.

A tear fell from Scully's eye.

"Fight him," Scully said quietly.

She saw Mulder's hand trembling and the cylinder of the pistol advancing slightly. There was a one-in-four chance she'd be dead in the next few seconds. Modell's eyes were shining. Sweat continued to pour from him, and he was trembling almost as much as Mulder. This was Modell's biggest challenge. The others he'd killed had only been a warm-up. He was proving himself superior to someone who'd always been in line ahead of him . . . to the best colleges . . . to the FBI . . . to the best of everything. He wasn't about to give up now. Instead, he pushed even harder.

"Come on!" he barked. "She shot *you* once. I read it in your file. Payback time! Shoot her!"

Scully couldn't keep looking at the gun pointing at her. Her eyes darted around the room. She didn't know what she was looking for: an escape, a weapon, something to shield herself. But she did know what it was when she found it. It was there in the mirror she was facing: a red fire alarm box on the wall directly behind her.

Mulder was using all his strength to keep from pulling the trigger. Another millimeter and it would be over. It felt, to Mulder, like trying to stay in a pushup position with somebody putting more and more weight on your back. Right now it felt like an elephant was up there. Mulder knew Modell would run out of strength soon. He just didn't know if it would be soon enough. He hated the man across the table from him for what he was and what he was making him do.

"I'm going to kill you, Modell," Mulder vowed, tears shining in his eyes.

"Yeah!" Modell enthused, almost as if the thought of that titillated him as much as watching Mulder point the gun at Scully. "Pull that trigger and you get another crack at me."

That sounded good to Mulder. If he got another crack at Modell, he wouldn't even fight it. He'd pull the trigger with gusto. But he couldn't let himself think that way. It meant shooting at Scully first, and that was a risk he didn't want to take. The elephant on his back was becoming a whale. He wasn't going to be able to hold on much longer.

"Run, Scully," Mulder said.

Scully began backing away, still facing Mulder.

"Scully . . . " Mulder whispered as he ratcheted the cylinder back . . . and back . . .

Scully spun and sprinted for the door. The fire alarm was on her way. She expected that at any instant she'd see her own blood on the wall in front of her, but Mulder held out. She reached her fingers into the casing of the alarm and yanked the white, T-shaped lever down as hard as she could.

Earsplitting sirens sounded throughout the hospital.

The noise caused Modell to take his eyes off Mulder and blink.

The weight that had been pressing down on Mulder fell away in the space of a heartbeat. He realized he didn't have to keep pointing the gun at Scully. The gun was now his to point at anyone he liked. He turned back and stared hard into Modell's eyes. He could see that Modell knew he had lost control.

In the split second before Mulder squeezed the trigger, he thought he saw the little man inside Pusher—afraid, cowering, helpless.

The first pull on the trigger did it. The bullet ripped a quarter-size hole in Modell's chest and propelled him out of the chair and onto the floor. Mulder stood and threw the table that had been between them out of the way. He approached Modell's body like a man possessed, gripped the pistol with both hands, aimed at Modell's head, and pulled the trigger again. There were no bullets left in the gun, but Mulder kept clicking through the empty chambers as the SWAT team flooded into the room.

"Federal agents! Get down! Get down!

Get down!" shouted Lieutenant Brophy. His men trained their automatic weapons on the heap at Mulder's feet as the deafening clang of the fire alarm rang through the hospital.

Mulder breathed in and out as though he'd just finished a marathon. The adrenaline slowly ebbed from his body. He sat back down in his original chair and closed his eyes, rubbed them. He held out the gun for Scully to take and wondered what he'd just done.

Chapter Sixteen

The rain had started a few hours after Mulder shot Modell. It fell cold and steady over the course of the day while Scully attempted to make a dent in the mountains of paperwork involved in wrapping up a case, especially one in which deadly force had been used. Mulder had gone home and tried to sleep, but he hadn't been successful. He'd just lain on his couch with his eyes wide open, staring at the drops of water that ran down the length of his windows. It hadn't been shooting Modell that bothered Mulder, though he'd never grown numb to the tragic responsibility of taking a man's life. The image that kept coming back into his head when he shut his eyes was of himself pointing that gun at Scully. He'd come so close to pulling the trigger. He knew he couldn't have held on another second. The look in Scully's eyes. Could she continue to be his partner? Would she ever trust him?

It was nearly ten o'clock when Mulder gave up and called her. He knew she'd be at her office. If there was one thing Scully couldn't stand, it was loose ends. She answered on the first ring.

"This is Scully."

"I want to see him," Mulder said.

Scully didn't have to ask who he was talking about.

"Can it wait until tomorrow?"

"I don't think so."

Scully looked at her watch and calculated distance and traffic. "I'll see you there in an hour."

"I'll wait for you at the emergency room entrance."

"All right," said Scully. "Forty minutes."

Mulder made it in thirty-eight. Scully arrived four minutes later. The hospital staff regarded the two FBI agents coolly as they folded their umbrellas and entered the foyer. Two of their own had lost their lives that day, and the consensus was that the feds had spent too much time playing war games in the parking lot. Why hadn't they simply marched right in? Maybe Rico and John would still be alive.

Modell was only three rooms down from where the standoff had taken place earlier in the day. He had a critical-care room to himself. An armed off-duty cop was reading the *Post* and guarding the door to Modell's room. He folded the paper when he saw the FBI agents approach.

Mulder and Scully flashed their badges. The cop pulled a key from his pocket and let the agents inside. Mulder waited until the door was shut behind him before speaking.

"Why the guard?"

"A number of people lost friends here today. It'd be pretty easy to 'accidentally' unplug the life support," Scully replied.

Mulder looked at Modell for the first time since entering.

Modell was still alive, but just barely. He was comatose, with myriad tubes routed into his body. Thick white bandages covered most of his face. A ventilator kept him breathing.

"There's no telling how long he'll hang on," Scully said, "but he'll never regain consciousness."

She looked across the foot of the bed at her partner. She was concerned for him. His expression was hard to read . . . even for her. He just kept staring at Modell. There was a long silence before Mulder spoke.

"You know, we thought he was undergoing treatment," he said. "We were wrong."

"What do you mean?"

"Read the chart," Mulder said. "The MRIs were a way to gauge how much life he had left. But he consistently refused treatment. His tumor remained operable up until the end. He refused to have it removed."

"Why?" Scully asked, surprised by the news.

"Like you said—he was a little man. It made him someone big."

"I say we don't let him take another minute of our time," Scully replied.

The slow rhythm of the ventilator filled the silence. Mulder didn't look well to Scully. He looked like someone who hadn't slept in a week, rather than the forty-eight hours she knew to be the case. Mulder stared at her, and for a moment, Scully was sure he was going to tell her something. Something important. But no words came out of his mouth. Scully wondered why it was so important that Mulder come down here tonight. She took a step toward her partner, and without looking down, took hold of Mulder's hand and squeezed.

Mulder pulled his eyes away from Modell and looked down at their hands. He squeezed back—tightly.

The End

Read the next book in the
X-Files Young Adult Series!

The X-Files #8: **The Host**

Chapter One

Dmitri Protemkin should have been a happy man. For as long as he could remember, he had wanted to go to sea. He grew up on a farm in Ukraine in the former Soviet Union. Standing in a sea of waving grain, he had looked longingly at the mighty river Dnieper flowing toward the Black Sea. Those fields of his childhood were plowed under after a nuclear reactor in nearby Chernobyl blew up. By that time Dmitri was away at school, training to be a ship's engineer. Then he got his first job. But his dream of riding the waves around the world turned out to be a nightmare.

Dmitri was the lowest-ranking engineer aboard an aging Russian cargo freighter. The ship was once called the *Lenin*. Then the Soviet Union fell apart, and the ship was renamed the *Liberty*. But the crew had their own name for her. They called her a floating garbage can.

Right now the *Liberty* was far from her home port of Vladivostok. Under stormy skies, she plowed through the dark Atlantic near the New Jersey coast. Dmitri could feel the ship bucking as she hit heavy swells. That was the only way he knew he was at sea. He lived below decks, slaving in the engine room, wolfing down greasy food in the galley, or sleeping like a log in his bunk. The last time he had seen the ocean was when he went topside to heave over the railing. At least by now he was no longer seasick. But still, life on the *Liberty* made farming look good. Dmitri was counting the days until the ship hit land and he could see trees and grass and smell fresh air again.

His shift for the day was almost over. Hauling a coil of rubber tubing, he climbed down an iron ladder to the smoke and din of the engine room. After he finished patching a leaky oil connection, he would be able to knock off.

He heard a voice booming over the engine noise, "Dmitri!"

Waiting for him was Serge Steklov, the ship's chief engineer. Serge's broad, bearded face wore a big smile.

Dmitri braced himself. He wondered what rotten new job Serge had for him. But before Serge could say a word, Dmitri said, "Sorry, I'm busy. The right lateral engine tubing needs to be replaced."

Serge's smile grew wider. "You worry too much," he told Dmitri. "Forget all that stuff you learned in school. The old tubing has lasted fifty years it will last a while longer."

"That's what they said about the Communist government until it collapsed," Dmitri said.

"Let us not waste time talking politics," Serge said. "We have a pressing problem. I have received a report that our toilets are backing up. We can do without our engines but not our toilets. We must see what we can do."

Dmitri grimaced. Serge said "we." But he meant one person alone.

"Follow me," Serge said.

He led Dmitri back up the ladder, then through a narrow corridor to the bathroom that the entire crew except the officers used. There, the two of them sloshed through brown water that had overflowed from the toilets.

"The whole system seems to be backing up," Serge said. "We'll have to investigate."

They left the bathroom, and went down another ladder into the depths of the ship. There a couple of crew members were grabbing quick forbidden smokes.

Serge ignored them as he tapped a square of metal plating on the bulkhead. "Behind this is the toilet disposal tank," he said. "We must find and remove whatever is in there blocking the system."

"Why is this always my job?" Dmitri griped.

Serge gave a hearty laugh, his big belly shaking.

"Because you are young," he told Dmitri. "And because it is terrible, smelly work."

As the two sailors joined in his laughter, he handed Dmitri a pneumatic drill.

Grimly Dmitri set to work removing the bolts that held the metal plate in place.

After ten minutes of sweaty work, Dmitri removed the plate.

He was almost knocked over by the odor that wafted out.

Standing well away from the opening, Serge said, "Go on, Dmitri. Take the plunge."

Dmitri turned his face away from the opening, and inhaled deeply. He held that breath as he reached in with a flashlight and stuck his head into the tank.

He played the light around the rippling filth, looking for the blockage. He leaned further in, hunting without success, until his air began to run out.

He was about to come out and take another breath when he spotted something.

Something slug-white and slimy.

Something like a hand.

Then an arm snaking out of the filth.

Then another hand and arm.

It was too late to pull back as the hands grabbed him around the neck and yanked him face forward toward the reeking stew.

Without thinking, he took a deep breath of the putrid air, then screamed.

Serge and the two other crew members rushed forward to grab Dmitri's kicking legs as his head was pulled under. They were big men, strong men but they were not big or strong enough to stop whatever it was they were up against.

Dmitri's body was ripped from their clutching hands and vanished through the opening.

The stench forgotten, Serge stuck his head into the tank, just in time to see the soles of Dmitri's workboots disappearing into the churning muck.

Then he saw a pale shape that made him jerk his head back and bellow to the bug-eyed sailors, "Flush the tanks! Flush the tanks!"

As they obeyed, he stared into the hole.

Only when he heard the roar of pumps emptying the storage tank into the sea did he breathe easier.

"Put the plate back in place," he commanded the sailors.

Then the chief engineer hurried back to the engine room. He didn't know what had been in the tank. He didn't want to know. He had grown up in a Russia where it was not healthy to ask what went on below the surface or what happened to people who disappeared. But one thing he did know. This ship should put as much distance as she could between herself and the gift she had just deposited on the doorstep of America.